Marvin's Friends

Written by Michèle Dufresne
Illustrated by Ann Caranci

PIONEER VALLEY EDUCATIONAL PRESS, INC.

Come and see
my friend the turtle.

3

Come and see
my friend the rabbit.

Come and see
my friend the cat.

Come and see
my friend the otter.

Come and see
my friend the dog.

Come and see
my friend the bird.

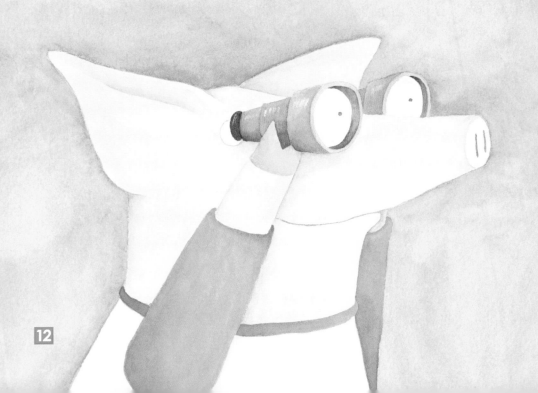

Come and see
my friend the monkey.

Come and see
my friend, Princess Pig!